THE OFFICIAL
BIRMINGHAM
CITY ANNUAL 2009

Written By Peter Oliver

A Grange Publication

© 2008. Published by Grange Communications Ltd., Edinburgh, under licence from Birmingham City Football Club.

Printed in the EU.

ISBN 978-1-906211-29-5

Photographs © Action Images

£6.99

FOUNDED 1875
HOME .... St. Andrew's
CAPACITY 30,009
CLUB NICKNAME .... Blues
MANAGER .... Alex McLeish
HONOURS

Football League Championship .... Promoted 2007
Division One .... Promoted 2001/02 (play-offs)
Division Two .... Champions 1892/93, 1920/21, 1947/48, 1954/55, 1994/95
Runners-up 1893/94, 1900/01, 1902/03, 1971/72, 1984/85
Division Three .... Runners-up 1991/92
FA Cup .... Runners-up 1931, 1956
League Cup .... Winners 1963, Runners-up 2001
Leyland Daf Cup .... Winners 1991
Auto Windscreens Shield .... Winners 1995
European Inter-Cities Fairs Cup .... Runners-up 1959/60, 1960/61
Record league goalscorer .... Joe Bradford (1920-35) 249
Most league appearances .... Frank Womack (1908-28) 491
Record league victory .... 12-0 v Walsall Town Swifts, December 1892

BIRMINGHAM CITY

CONTENTS 2009

INTRODUCTION

WELCOME TO THE 2009 BIRMINGHAM CITY ANNUAL.

This season is my first full season as manager of Birmingham City and in many ways it is a fresh start. We would have loved to have stayed up last season but despite a decent enough points total from December onwards we couldn't quite do it.

The summer saw lots of changes in personnel on and off the field. This has given us the chance to put together a new-look squad which we hope will be able to challenge for promotion.

The Championship will be a tough league to get out of and it will take a concerted effort from everyone from management, staff, players and supporters to make the impact we hope. Having had another taste of the Premier League last season that's where we all want Blues to be.

We'll all be giving it our best shot and I hope you enjoy the ride. Enjoy the annual and here's to a successful 2008/09 season.

Alex McLeish

THE BOSS: ALEX McLEISH
BRAVEHEART

When the Blues went looking for their first new manager in six years, their search took them north of the border to land one of the most successful managers in recent Scottish football history – Alex McLeish.

It was all change in the managerial hot-seat at St. Andrew's during the 2007/08 campaign as Steve Bruce's departure made way for the arrival of Alex McLeish.

When Bruce left at the end of November to join Wigan Athletic for a second time it meant the end of an era for the Blues.

The former Manchester United defender had spent almost six years as the Blues boss after earlier spells in charge of Crystal Palace, Huddersfield and Sheffield United.

Bruce twice led the Blues to promotion to the Premier League in a successful stay in the Midlands and when he left following uncertainty over a new contract, the board looked to repeat the formula by going for another man schooled by the best in the business – Alex Ferguson.

Like Bruce, McLeish enjoyed considerable playing success under Ferguson, although his silverware was won at Aberdeen when the Dons broke the stranglehold on success of the Glasgow giants Rangers and Celtic.

McLeish formed a powerful central defensive unit at Pittodrie alongside club captain Willie Miller as Aberdeen won three Scottish League titles, four Scottish Cups, two League Cups, the European Cup Winners' Cup and the European Super Cup – all but two of them under Ferguson who has remained a close friend and mentor of the Blues new boss.

McLeish had earlier studied to be an accountant and he needed a head for figures as he racked up some 600 games for Aberdeen, as well as playing 77 times for Scotland, making him the third most capped player in Scottish history and taking him to the World Cup finals three times.

'Big Eck', as the Blues manager is known, used his playing education well as he smoothly made the transition into management with Motherwell in 1994, spending four years at Fir Park before moving to Edinburgh to take control at Hibernian.

Inheriting a struggling team, McLeish could not prevent Hibs being relegated from the Scottish Premier League, but in an omen the Blues fans hope will be repeated, he led them to an instant return with promotion at the first attempt.

He guided them up to third place in the SPL and a Scottish Cup final to attract the attention of Rangers, who appointed him as their manager in December, 2001.

In his first season at Ibrox Park, Rangers won a domestic cup double and the following year they made it a treble by also adding the Scottish League title.

In 2005 Rangers were champions again and then qualified for the last-16 of the Champions League before McLeish's reign came to an end in 2006.

With that track record of success there was only one job left for McLeish in Scotland and the opportunity to manage the national team came in January 2007 when Walter Smith returned to Rangers.

Picking up where Smith had left off, McLeish inspired the Scots to some remarkable results, notably a win over France in Paris that took them to the brink of qualification for the finals of Euro 2008.

Sadly the Scots' dreams were dashed with a home defeat by Italy in their final group game, and when the Blues approached the Scottish FA in pursuit of a new manager in late November, 2007, McLeish answered the call to resume his club career with a new challenge in English football at St. Andrew's.

The first part of that challenge was to try and keep the Blues in the Premier League. But after inheriting a Blues team that had taken just 11 points from the first 14 games, it was a task that proved just beyond McLeish and his powers of recovery.

Under the Scot, the Blues won a further 24 points from 24 games but were consigned to the drop on the final day of the season.

McLeish immediately pledged to put his own stamp on the club, and after a summer of frantic transfer activity he will be looking to guide 'his team' to promotion at the first attempt and get the Blues back where they belong – in the Premier League.

He said: "When you look at some of the names in the Championship that have been in the Premier League before it's actually quite frightening so there are no guarantees for us."

"But if I can get players of the ilk of Phillips and Carsley, combined with a lot of the players we already have here, then I would be very confident we can be a force."

SEASON REVIEW 2007/08

Blues return to the top flight sadly lasted just one season but 2007/08 was still full of drama. Relive the Blues' life in the Premier League as the season unfolded. Hopefully it won't be long before Alex McLeish's men are back

AUGUST

Chelsea 3, Birmingham City 2

Birmingham City 2, Sunderland 2

Birmingham City 0, West Ham 1

Derby County 1, Birmingham City 2

Birmingham City 2, Hereford United 1 (Carling Cup)

Steve Bruce's new-look team couldn't have been given a tougher start to life back in the big time as they were handed an opening day trip to defending champions Chelsea. Ultimately Blues couldn't prevent Chelsea breaking Liverpool's league record of 63 unbeaten home games but Jose Mourinho's men were given a fright at Stamford Bridge. Mikael Forssell scored against his former club to give the Blues the lead and a stunning strike from debut boy Olivier Kapo made it 2-2 before Michael Essien bagged all three points for the Londoners.

A first win of the campaign was then snatched from Blues grasp when Sunderland escaped from St. Andrew's with a draw thanks to a last-gasp leveller from old boy Stern John after Garry O'Connor looked like his debut goal

had clinched victory. More disappointment was then to follow as West Ham collected a controversial win thanks to a debatable penalty claimed by Craig Bellamy, who went down under goalkeeper Colin Doyle's challenge, and netted by Mark Noble.

Doyle lost his place to Maik Taylor for Blues trip to Derby and the veteran keeper ended up on the winning side, as the Blues opened their account thanks to a double blast from Cameron Jerome, as hapless Derby were given a taste of things to come. Bruce made a further change between the posts in the Carling Cup as Richard Kingson made an impressive debut in a much-changed side which edged out Hereford United, thanks to goals from O'Connor and Gary McSheffrey to progress to round two.

SEPTEMBER

Middlesbrough 2, Birmingham City 0
Birmingham City 1, Bolton Wanderers 0
Liverpool 0, Birmingham City 0
Blackburn Rovers 3, Birmingham City 0 (Carling Cup)
Birmingham City 0, Manchester United 1

Any hopes of putting together a winning run were dashed on Teesside at the start of September, but the Blues swiftly bounced back by recording a first home league win of the season against early strugglers Bolton.

Olivier Kapo continued his impressive start in a Blues shirt with the only goal as a first clean sheet of the campaign guaranteed maximum points and lifted the Blues close to mid-table as the league began to take shape.

Another magnificent defensive display at Anfield maintained Blues momentum as in-form Liverpool were held to a goalless draw, but any hopes of a decent run in the Carling Cup were dashed by a comprehensive defeat at Blackburn.

Resting so many players at Ewood Park was partially justified as Blues then turned in an impressive performance against Manchester United but a Cristiano Ronaldo goal was still enough to give the would-be champions the narrowest of victories at St. Andrew's.

OCTOBER

Blackburn Rovers 2, Birmingham City 1
Manchester City 1, Birmingham City 0
Birmingham City 3, Wigan Athletic 2

Blues made a rapid return to Lancashire to take on Blackburn and suffered a repeat of their cup defeat as their long winless streak at Ewood Park continued.

Goals from David Bentley and Bennie McCarthy, from the spot, gave Rovers the breathing space to survive a Cameron Jerome goal as the Blues paid the price for earlier missed chances.

Goals were again in short supply when Manchester City handed out a third straight defeat courtesy of Brazilian Elano, which had Steve Bruce spitting feathers after the Blues were denied a free-kick in the run-up to the goal.

However, the rot was stopped with a thrilling 3-2 victory over Wigan Athletic, which was ultimately to have major repercussions for both olubo.

Wigan, who were tumbling down the table, twice led through Marcus Bent, but the Blues pegged them back through an Olivier Kapo penalty and Liam Ridgewell's first goal for the club, before Kapo rammed home the winner nine minutes from the end.

NOVEMBER

Everton 3, Birmingham City 1
Birmingham City 1, Aston Villa 2
Birmingham City 0, Portsmouth 2

November proved to be a disastrous month in which Blues failed to take a point and also lost manager Steve Bruce.

Things started badly as two late goals from Everton gave the Toffees a 3-1 win on Merseyside. Olivier Kapo's header looked to have earned the Blues a point but a rare goal from Lee Carsley, later to become a Blues player, and a second in injury-time from James Vaughan scuppered those hopes.

A derby clash against Aston Villa offered the possibility of an instant remedy, but Villa only rubbed salt into the wounds with a 2-1 win at St. Andrew's. Former Villa man Ridgewell diverted a Stiliyan Petrov cross into his own goal to give the visitors the lead, and although substitute Mikael Forssell levelled, Villa stole the points thanks to a late header from Gabriel Agbonlahor, which made a sorry ending to Bruce's near six-year reign as Blues' boss.

Bruce's departure left Eric Black in temporary charge but his sole game as caretaker-manager also ended in defeat.

Black selected Richard Kingson for a Premier League debut, but a mistake by the Ghanaian goalkeeper helped Pompey lead before a late goal from Niko Kranjcar confirmed a sixth defeat in seven games, which left Blues hovering just above the drop zone.

DECEMBER

Tottenham Hotspur 2, Birmingham City 3
Newcastle United 2, Birmingham City 1
Birmingham City 1, Reading 1
Bolton 3, Birmingham City 0
Birmingham City 3, Middlesbrough 0
Birmingham City 1, Fulham 1

The appointment of Alex McLeish as Bruce's successor had an immediate effect as a spectacular late strike from Sebastian Larsson got the Blues back to winning ways in dramatic fashion at White Hart Lane.

Gary McSheffrey got the McLeish era up and running when he opened the scoring from the penalty spot, but two goals from Robbie Keane threatened to spoil the party.

Keane's afternoon was cut short by a red card, though, after Cameron Jerome had equalised, and with Spurs down to ten men they were rocked in injury-time when Super Swede Larsson lashed a 35-yarder past Paul Robinson to bag the points.

The tables were turned a week later when Habib Beye's late goal gave Newcastle victory at St. James' Park after Jerome had struck early for the Blues, but McLeish was then able to celebrate his first point at St. Andrew's when an early Mikael Forssell goal produced a stalemate with Reading.

Any thoughts that Blues had completely turned the corner were soon dismissed at Bolton where a 3-0 defeat brought little Christmas cheer for the Blues' fans, but there was a belated gift in the shape of a similarly convincing home win over Middlesbrough on Boxing Day.

Stewart Downing overdid the seasonal generosity with an own-goal before another Forssell strike and a late Gary McSheffrey penalty sent the supporters home happy.

Unfortunately, though, they were not to enjoy the winning feeling again for more than two months as Fulham brought the curtain down on 2007 with a 1-1 draw at St. Andrew's, Larsson equalising as the Blues reached the turn of the year 15th in the table – three points clear of the relegation places.

SEASON REVIEW 07/08

JANUARY

Manchester United 1, Birmingham City 0
Huddersfield Town 2, Birmingham City 1 (FA Cup)
Arsenal 1, Birmingham City 1
Birmingham City 0, Chelsea 1
Sunderland 2, Birmingham City 0

A trip to Old Trafford made a happy New Year unlikely and while there was no shame in going down to a Carlos Tevez goal, Blues FA Cup exit at League One side Huddersfield Town was a worrying sign of things to come. Garry O'Connor's equaliser looked as though it would spare the Blues' blushes but a late goal from Chris Brandon gave the underdogs a deserved victory and left Blues with just a relegation fight to look forward to.

They at least tackled that with relish at Arsenal as a headed equaliser from O'Connor helped the Blues – with captain Damien Johnson back in a face mask to protect the skull fracture sustained against Fulham – become only the second team so fro to deny joint league leaders Arsenal maximum points.

However, the fixtures did not get any easier, and despite another battling performance, a late goal from Chelsea's Claudio Pizarro next up made it a losing start for new Blues signing James McFadden, who made his debut from the bench.

And a disappointing defeat away to Sunderland at the end of the month meant only goal difference was keeping the Blues out of the dreaded bottom-three.

FEBRUARY

Birmingham City 1, Derby County 1
West Ham United 1, Birmingham City 1
Birmingham City 2, Arsenal 2

Billed as a 'must-win' game, the Blues could only manage a draw against doomed Derby with Sebastian Larsson's goal being cancelled out late on by Emanuel Villa.

Former Hibernian full-back David Murphy made his Blues debut after recovering from injury, but there was little else to enthuse over as results elsewhere sent McLeish's men into the relegation zone as the battle for survival began to hot up. Every result meant a nervous look at the league table, but at least James McFadden's first goal for the club at West Ham, scored from the penalty spot, offered a glimmer of hope as Blues moved up a place.

McFadden's value to Blues was further underlined with a double blast against table-topping Arsenal as the Blues proved they would not go down without a fight. The Scotland international scored with a delightful free-kick and an injury-time penalty, but the gloss of a hard-earned point with ten men was taken off by the injury sustained by Arsenal forward Eduardo. The Brazilian-born Croatian international suffered a broken leg and dislocated ankle after being caught by the Blues defender Martin Taylor, whose mis-timed tackle brought a red card and more than his fair share of un-merited criticism.

MARCH

Blues achieved the biggest win of the season by thrashing Tottenham. Sebastian Larsson scored another memorable goal, this time from a free-kick, but it was Mikael Forssell's day as the top-scorer claimed his first ever hat-trick at club level to give Blues their first win since Boxing Day.

But just when Blues needed a run to propel themselves clear of relegation trouble, their wretched away form cost them dearly. Despite fighting back from 2-0 down at Portsmouth through Fabrice Muamba's first Blues' goal and dead-ball king Larsson, Blues shipped two second half goals on the south coast to spark a disastrous run of five successive away defeats.

Michael Owen then eased the pressure on Newcastle manager Kevin Keegan when he stopped McFadden from giving Alex McLeish a much-needed win of his own, and there was to be little respite for the Blues boss when his side then lost at relegation rivals Reading. Mauro Zarate's first goal in a Blues shirt gave a tantalising glimpse of what was to come, but conceding two goals from set-pieces proved highly damaging.

Zarate had signed on loan from Qatar club Al-Sadd in January but really burst onto the scene in the spring, and his two clinically taken goals against Manchester City, along with a Gary McSheffrey penalty, seemed to breathe new life into the Blues' survival campaign as they overcame the dismissal of Franck Queudrue.

SEASON REVIEW 07/08

APRIL

Wigan Athletic 2, Birmingham City 0
Birmingham City 1, Everton 1
Aston Villa 5, Birmingham City 1
Birmingham City 2, Liverpool 2

Blues had a four point cushion above the bottom-three going into April but by the end of a pivotal month without a win they were back in the drop-zone.

Things started badly at Wigan where Steve Bruce put one over his former club thanks to a double from Ryan Taylor and a red card for the Blues captain Damien Johnson.

And another goal from Mauro Zarate was only enough to salvage a point against Everton at St. Andrew's as the Argentina under-20 international curled home a stunning late free-kick.

Blues then hit rock-bottom with a 5-1 mauling at local rivals Aston Villa, with Mikael Forssell's second-half goal no consolation for a crushing defeat that left McLeish fuming.

With little margin for error in the race to avoid an instant return to the Championship, Blues looked to have repaired some of the damage when they set about restoring lost pride against Liverpool.

Goals from the deadly duo of Forssell and Sebastian Larsson had McLeish's men cruising ten minutes into the second half. But disaster then struck when Peter Crouch and Yossi Benayoun netted for Liverpool, the equaliser coming from a cruel deflection past Maik Taylor to sum up the Blues plight.

MAY

Fulham 2, Birmingham City 0
Birmingham City 4, Blackburn Rovers 1

With two games left to save themselves, the Blues had to travel to London to take on a resurgent Fulham side that was pursuing its own great escape.

And with the momentum behind them, it was the Cottagers who dealt the almost fatal blow to the Blues hopes of staying up.

The Blues had no answer to second-half goals from Brian McBride and Erik Nevland, which meant that their destiny was no longer in their own hands going into the final day of the season as they slipped to second from bottom of the table.

McLeish's side now had to win against Blackburn and hope that results went their way to preserve their top-flight status.

But despite managing the first half of the equation with a thumping 4-1 victory, thanks to goals from Cameron Jerome, two, David Murphy and Fabrice Muamba, Fulham's victory at Portsmouth consigned both Blues and Reading to the drop along with Derby.

The roller-coaster ride ended in despair as Blues were relegated for the second time in three seasons.

DAMIEN
JOHNSON

Premier League
Table 2007/08

POS	CLUB	Pld	HOME					AWAY					TOTAL					GD	PTS
			W	D	L	F	A	W	D	L	F	A	W	D	L	F	A		
1	Manchester United	38	17	1	1	47	7	10	5	4	33	15	27	6	5	80	22	58	87
2	Chelsea	38	12	7	0	36	13	13	3	3	29	13	25	10	3	65	26	39	85
3	Arsenal	38	14	5	0	37	11	10	6	3	37	20	24	11	3	74	31	43	83
4	Liverpool	38	12	6	1	43	13	9	7	3	24	15	21	13	4	67	28	39	76
5	Everton	38	11	4	4	34	17	8	4	7	21	16	19	8	11	55	33	22	65
6	Aston Villa	38	10	3	6	34	22	6	9	4	37	29	16	12	10	71	51	20	60
7	Blackburn Rovers	38	8	7	4	26	19	7	6	6	24	29	15	13	10	50	48	2	58
8	Portsmouth	38	7	8	4	24	14	9	1	9	24	26	16	9	13	48	40	8	57
9	Manchester City	38	11	4	4	28	20	4	6	9	17	33	15	10	13	45	53	-8	55
10	West Ham United	38	7	7	5	24	24	6	3	10	18	26	13	10	15	42	50	-8	49
11	Tottenham Hotspur	38	8	5	6	46	34	3	8	8	20	27	11	13	14	66	61	5	46
12	Newcastle United	38	8	5	6	25	26	3	5	11	20	39	11	10	17	45	65	-20	43
13	Middlesbrough	38	7	5	7	27	23	3	7	9	16	30	10	12	16	43	53	-10	42
14	Wigan Athletic	38	8	5	6	21	17	2	5	12	13	34	10	10	18	34	51	-17	40
15	Sunderland	38	9	3	7	23	21	2	3	14	13	38	11	6	21	36	59	-23	39
16	Bolton Wanderers	38	7	5	7	23	18	2	5	12	13	36	9	10	19	36	54	-18	37
17	Fulham	38	5	5	9	22	31	3	7	9	16	29	8	12	18	38	60	-22	36
18	Reading	38	8	2	9	19	25	2	4	13	22	41	10	6	22	41	66	-25	36
19	Birmingam City	38	6	8	5	30	23	2	3	14	16	39	8	11	19	46	62	-16	35
20	Derby County	38	1	5	13	12	43	0	3	16	8	46	1	8	29	20	89	-69	11

Birmingham City
Appearances and goals 2007/08

Player						
S Aluko	0 (0)	0	0 (0)	0	0 (1)	0
N Danns	0 (2)	0	0 (0)	0	2 (0)	0
D De Ridder	6 (4)	0	1 (0)	0	1 (0)	0
J Djourou	13 (0)	0	0 (0)	0	0 (0)	0
C Doyle	3 (0)	0	0 (1)	0	0 (1)	0
M Forssell	21 (9)	9	1 (0)	0	1 (0)	0
D Howland	0 (0)	0	0 (0)	0	0 (0)	0
R Jaidi	18 (0)	0	1 (0)	0	1 (0)	0
C Jerome	21 (12)	7	0 (1)	0	0 (0)	0
D Johnson	17 (0)	0	0 (0)	0	1 (0)	0
O Kapo	22 (4)	5	0 (0)	0	1 (0)	0
S Kelly	38 (0)	0	1 (0)	0	1 (0)	0
R Kingson	1 (0)	0	0 (0)	0	2 (0)	0
Maik Taylor	34 (0)	0	1 (0)	0	0 (0)	0
Martin Taylor	4 (0)	0	0 (0)	0	1 (0)	0
J McFadden	10 (2)	4	0 (0)	0	0 (0)	0
G McSheffrey	24 (8)	3	1 (0)	0	1 (0)	1
B Melendez	1 (1)	0	0 (0)	0	0 (0)	0
F Muamba	37 (0)	2	1 (0)	0	0 (0)	0
D Murphy	14 (0)	1	0 (0)	0	0 (0)	0
J Mutch	0 (0)	0	0 (0)	0	0 (0)	0
M Nafti	19 (7)	0	0 (0)	0	1 (0)	0
G O'Connor	5 (18)	2	1 (0)	1	2 (0)	1
W Palacios	4 (3)	0	0 (0)	0	0 (1)	0
S Parnaby	4 (9)	0	0 (0)	0	2 (0)	0
K Pearce	0 (0)	0	0 (0)	0	0 (0)	0
F Queudrue	14 (2)	0	0 (0)	0	1 (0)	0
L Ridgewell	35 (0)	1	1 (0)	0	1 (0)	0
M Sadler	3 (2)	0	0 (0)	0	2 (0)	0
R Schmitz	12 (3)	0	0 (0)	0	0 (1)	0
S Larsson	32 (3)	6	1 (0)	0	1 (0)	0
R Vine	0 (0)	0	0 (0)	0	2 (0)	0
M Zarate	6 (8)	4	0 (0)	0	0 (0)	0

Sun 12 Aug	Chelsea	A	League	L 2-3	Forssell 15; Kapo 36	41590
Wed 15 Aug	Sunderland	H	League	D 2-2	McShane 28og; O'Connor 82	24898
Sat 18 Aug	West Ham Utd.	H	League	L 0-1		24961
Sat 25Aug	Derby County	A	League	W 2-1	Jerome 1, 63	31117
Tue 28 Aug	Hereford Utd.	H	League Cup	W 2-1	O'Connor 27; McSheffrey 38	10185
Sat 01 Sep	Middlesbrough	A	League	L 0-2		22920
Sat 15 Sep	Bolton	H	League	W 1-0	Kapo 37	28124
Sat 22 Sep	Liverpool	A	League	D 0-0		44215
Wed 26 Sep	Blackburn	A	League Cup	L 0-3		9205
Sat 29 Sep	Man Utd.	H	League	L 0-1		26526
Sun 07 Oct	Blackburn	A	League	L 1-2	Jerome 68	19316
Sat 20 Oct	Man City	A	League	L 0-1		45688
Sat 27 Oct	Wigan Athletic	H	League	W 3-2	Kapo 26p, 81; Ridgemell 67	27661
Sat 03 Nov	Everton	A	League	L 1-3	Kapo 80	34155
Sun 11 Nov	Aston Villa	H	League	L 1-2	Forssell 62	26539
Sat 24 Nov	Portsmouth	H	League	L 0-2		22089
Sun 02 Dec	Tottenham HS	H	League	W 3-2	McSheffrey 24p; Jerome 62; Larsson 90	35635
Sat 08 Dec	Newcastle Utd.	A	League	L 1-2	Jermone 9	49948
Sat 15 Dec	Reading	H	League	D 1-1	Forssell 4	27300
Sat 22 Dec	Bolton	A	League	L 0-3		19111
Wed 26 Dec	Middlesbrough	H	League	W 3-0	Downing 22og; Forssell 45; McSheffrey 90p	24094
Sat 29 Dec	Fulham	H	League	D 1-1	Larsson 55	28923
Tue 01 Jan	Man Utd.	A	League	L 0-1		75459
Sat 05 Jan	Huddersfield	A	F.A. Cup	L 1-2	O'Connor 19	13410
Sat 12 Jan	Arsenal	A	League	D 1-1	O'Connor 48	60037
Sat 19 Jan	Chelsea	H	League	L 0-1		26567
Tue 29 Jan	Sunderland	A	League	L 0-2		37674
Sat 02 Feb	Derby County	H	League	D 1-1	Larsson 68	25924
Sat 09 Feb	West Ham Utd.	A	League	D 1-1	McFadden 16p	34884
Sat 23 Feb	Arsenal	H	League	D 2-2	McFadden 28, 90p	27185
Sat 01 Mar	Tottenham HS	H	League	W 4-1	Forssell 7, 59, 81; Larsson 55	26055
Wed 12 Mar	Portsmouth	A	League	L 2-4	Muamba 10; Larsson 40	20138
Mon 17 Mar	Newcastle Utd.	H	League	D 1-1	McFadden 33	25777
Sat 22 Mar	Reading	A	League	L 1-2	Zarate 64	24085
Sat 29 Mar	Man City	H	League	W 3-1	Zarate 40, 54; McSheffrey 77p	22962
Sat 05 Apr	Wigan	A	League	L 0-2		17926
Sat 12 Apr	Everton	H	League	D 1-1	Zarate 83	25923
Sun 20 Apr	Aston Villa	A	League	L 1-5	Forssell 67	42640
Sat 26 Apr	Liverpool	H	League	D 2-2	Forssell 34; Larsson 55	29252
Sat 03 May	Fulham	A	League	L 0-2		25308
Sun 11 May	Blackburn	H	League	W 4-1	Murphy 31; Jerome 73, 89; Muamba 90	26668

CAMERON
JEROME

GOALS OF THE SEASON
SIX OF THE BEST

There wasn't too much for the Blues fans to cheer about last season, but among the highlights were some fantastic goals. Here are six of the best:

Pride of place goes to Sebastian Larsson's stunning, long-range match-winner against Tottenham at White Hart Lane in December which gave Alex McLeish a winning start to his Blues reign and earned the Super Swede the goal of the season award.

Larsson made a habit of scoring spectacular goals and earned another entry for this superb free-kick against Liverpool in April which raised the Blues hopes of staying in the Premier League.

James McFadden really announced his arrival as a Blues player with a double against Arsenal to earn the Blues a 2-2 draw at St. Andrew's in February. His first was a perfectly placed free-kick which he curled past the defensive wall and goalkeeper Manuel Almunia.

Mikael Forssell might have scored more thrilling goals during his five seasons with the Blues, but few will have meant more than the third he scored against Tottenham at St. Andrew's in March when he became the first Blues player to score a hat-trick in the Premier League.

On-loan striker Mauro Zarate lit up the Blues fight against the drop as he hit a late burst of form and scored four goals in four games to give Alex McLeish's side a glimmer of hope. The young Argentinian's first home goals came against Manchester City, including this neat finish past City keeper Joe Hart.

Blues announced their presence in the top flight by pushing champions Chelsea all the way on the opening day at Stamford Bridge with this thunderbolt from Olivier Kapo levelling the scores.

The Blues may be back in the Championship but they will still face plenty of former Premier League opponents in their quest to win an instant return to the top-flight.

No fewer than 14 of their rivals have played in the Premier League before, which gives a clue as to the tough task the Blues will face.

Alex McLeish's men started out among the favourites for promotion, but the Blues boss knows that, and his club's recent achievements will mark them out as a target.

"Every team we come up against throughout the season will want to beat us," McLeish said.

"Many of them will see us as a real scalp if they can get one over us and it's our job to make sure that doesn't happen.

"Every game in the Championship is a big challenge but they are all challenges we are really looking forward to."

The Blues have lost their big second city derby against fierce rivals Aston Villa, while West Bromwich Albion's promotion has also deprived them of another all-Midlands clash.

But the Blues' fans will have pencilled in the two games against Wolves as ones to look forward to, while the promotion of former European champions, Nottingham Forest, makes for two more tasty clashes.

And if there is anything riding on the last day of the season, all eyes will be on a trip to Reading, who are also looking to make amends for last season's relegation disappointment.

FIXTURES 2008/09

The Blues Championship 2008/09 fixtures
(fixtures are subject to change)

AUGUST

Saturday 9	Sheffield United (h)
Wednesday 13	Wycombe Wanderers (a) (CarlingCup)
Saturday 16	Southampton (a)
Saturday 23	Barnsley (h)
Saturday 30	Norwich City (a)

SEPTEMBER

Saturday 13	Doncaster Rovers (h)
Tuesday 16	Bristol City (a)
Saturday 20	Blackpool (h)
Saturday 27	Cardiff City (a)
Tuesday 30	Derby County (a)

OCTOBER

Saturday 4	QPR (h)
Saturday 18	Burnley (a)
Tuesday 21	Crystal Palace (h)
Saturday 25	Sheffield Wednesday (h)
Tuesday 28	QPR (a)

NOVEMBER

Monday 3	Coventry City (h)
Saturday 8	Nottingham Forest (a)
Saturday 15	Charlton Athletic (h)
Friday 21	Swansea City (a)
Tuesday 25	Ipswich Town (h)
Saturday 29	Wolverhampton Wanderers (a)

DECEMBER

Saturday 6	Watford (h)
Tuesday 9	Plymouth Argyle (a)
Saturday 13	Preston (a)
Saturday 20	Reading (h)
Friday 26	Ipswich Town (a)
Sunday 28	Swansea City (h)

JANUARY 2009

Saturday 10	Blackpool (a)
Saturday 17	Cardiff City (h)
Tuesday 27	Derby County (h)
Saturday 31	Sheffield Wednesday (a)

FEBRUARY

Tuesday 3	Crystal Palace (a)
Saturday 7	Burnley (h)
Saturday 14	Nottingham Forest (h)
Saturday 21	Coventry City (a)
Saturday 28	Sheffield United (a)

MARCH

Tuesday 3	Bristol City (h)
Saturday 7	Southampton (h)
Tuesday 10	Barnsley (a)
Saturday 14	Doncaster Rovers (a)
Saturday 21	Norwich City (h)

APRIL

Saturday 4	Wolves (h)
Saturday 11	Charlton (a)
Monday 13	Plymouth Argyle (h)
Saturday 18	Watford (a)
Saturday 25	Preston (h)

MAY

Sunday 3	Reading (a)

GARRY
O'CONNOR

BIG
BLUES QUIZ

LET'S GET QUIZZICAL!

Test your Blues knowledge in this fun quiz:

1 Which management job did Alex McLeish have before taking charge of the Blues?

2 Who was the Blues top scorer in the Premier League in the 2007/08 season?

3 Which Blues player took part in Euro 2008?

4 Can you name the two other clubs in the Midlands new Blues striker Kevin Phillips has played for?

5 Which country does new Blues midfielder Lee Carsley play for?

6 Where did the Blues go for their pre-season tour in the summer?

7 Which player played in every minute of all the Blues Premier League games in the 2007/08 season?

8 New striker Marcus Bent scored for which team against the Blues last season?

9 David Murphy joined the Blues from Hibernian, but which English club did he previously play for?

10 Who is the oldest player in the Blues first-team squad?

11 What is the name of the Blues training ground?

12 Who signed for the Blues last season in a deal which could rise to be a club record?

Answers page 61

29

KING KEV

"It's all about creating the chances and with the players we've got here I'm sure they'll create chances in this league."

The Blues underlined their determination to challenge for promotion when they swooped to sign goal-machine Kevin Phillips from neighbours West Bromwich Albion.

The former England international bagged 24 goals last season to spearhead the Baggies' Championship title success.

His phenomenal career record and hunger to keep hitting the net meant the Blues boss, Alex McLeish, had no hesitation in handing the 34-year-old a two-year deal in the summer.

Capped eight times by his country, 'Super Kev' also tasted promotion to the top flight with Sunderland and has a pedigree second to none at Championship level.

A career tally of 235 goals with Watford, Sunderland, Southampton, Aston Villa and West Brom says it all for the pint-sized striker who topped the Premier League scoring charts in 1999/2000 when his 30 goals for Sunderland won him the Golden

Boot as Europe's top marksman.
The Blues fans can now enjoy watching one of the best strikers of his generation at St Andrew's and Phillips is determined not to disappoint them.

"I'd love to be part of a Birmingham team that gained promotion and be up there as top goal scorer again," he said.

"I've proved I can do it over the last two years and there's no reason I can't do it this year."

Phillips added: "It's all about creating the chances and with the players we've got here I'm sure they'll create chances in this league.

"I'm looking forward to helping this club try and gain promotion as I did at West Brom."

FACT FILE

Name: Kevin Phillips
Born: 25 July, 1973, Hitchin
Position: Striker
Previous clubs: Watford, Sunderland, Southampton, Aston Villa, West Bromich Albion
Career goals: 235
International caps: 8

YOUNG GUNS

While the Blues look for an instant return to Premier League football with some proven performers in their ranks, they also have an eye on the future in the shape of emerging young talent at St. Andrew's. The Blues Academy and scouting network is responsible for nurturing potential stars and here are four to look out for.

KRYSTIAN PEARCE

JORDON MUTCH

While the Blues started their warm-up for the new season, Pearce was in action for England under-19s in the European Championships as he continued his eye-catching development. A powerful centre-half, Pearce should learn much from the Blues' boss, Alex McLeish, who was one of the best in the business in his position. McLeish would be a tough act to follow but since emerging from the St. Andrew's Academy, Pearce has made rapid strides to suggest that he has what it takes to make the grade at first-team level. After progressing into the Blues' reserve side his performances caught the eye of League clubs and he made 20 appearances for Notts County and Port Vale during loan spells in 2007/08. With that kind of experience under his belt, forcing his way into McLeish's first-team plans may not be too far away after Pearce signed a new two-year contract in May.

The midfielder, 17 in December, was signed from Derby County in the summer of 2007, but despite his tender age, was given a squad number last season. He was even included in the Blues squad to play Blackburn Rovers in the Carling Cup but could not play as he was just 15 at the time. Progressing in the reserves last season, the Academy scholar joined the Blues on their pre-season trip to Austria to suggest he could have a part to play in the Championship this season. "He is a really good, young professional who goes about his business in the right manner," said first-team coach Roy Aitken. "He has got good potential but like any other player he has to keep working hard and doing the right things."

JARED WILSON

SONE ALUKO

A second-year professional who has come through the ranks at St. Andrew's, Wilson is a lively full-back who is also looking to make the break-through at first-team level.

Wilson agreed a new contract in the summer after appearing in around half of the Blues reserve-team fixtures last season.

And after earning a place in the Blues pre-season training camp, the 19-year-old faced a big year, according to manager Alex McLeish.

Well known as an exciting prospect through his lengthy stay at the Blues Academy, this could be the year the dynamic striker comes of age. An England international at under-15 to under-19 age groups, Aluko was given an extended taste of senior football in 2007/08 with a season-long loan at Aberdeen. A handful of goals for the Scottish Premier League side suggest that he may be ready to add to his solitary senior appearance for Blues. Competition for places among the strikers in Alex McLeish's squad will be fierce but Aluko, whose sister is an England international, will be champing at the bit for a chance to prove he can cut it in the Championship.

"I'm not looking to wind down my career. I'm looking to play in the Premier League and I want to do it with Birmingham."

The Blues might have been relegated last season, but they still have Premier League pedigree in their ranks as the arrival of midfield man Lee Carsley proved.

Carsley ended a six-year stay in the top-flight with Everton to return to his home city and join Alex McLeish's St. Andrew's revolution - starting the season as the new team captain.

And the Republic of Ireland international made it clear that he has not given up on returning to the top tier during his time with the Blues.

"We'll be looking to get promoted. That's everybody's goal," said Carsley, who was McLeish's first new signing ahead of the current campaign.

"If everybody is pulling in the right way there's no reason why we can't achieve it."

"I'm not looking to wind down my career. I'm looking to play in the Premier League and I want to do it with Birmingham."

"I'm aware of that fact that I've not won anything in my career. I've come here to win a Championship and stabilise the club in the Premier League."

Carsley may not have any silverware to show for his efforts, but he has previously tasted promotion from the Championship with Derby County and twice helped Everton to top-five finishes in the Premier League.

A holding midfield player capped 39 times by Ireland, the Birmingham-born player always gives total commitment and will bring some vital steel and authority to the Blues' midfield as they look to complete the marathon that is the Championship promotion race.

FACT FILE

Name: Lee Carsley
Born: 28 February, 1974, Birmingham
Position: Midfielder
Previous clubs: Derby, Blackburn, Coventry, Everton
Career club goals: 466
International caps: 39

BACKROOM BOYS

Playing at St. Andrew's, it is fitting that the Blues now have a strong Scottish flavour thanks to their management team.

When former Scotland defender and national team boss Alex McLeish was appointed he brought in a backroom staff also steeped in the tartan tradition.

First-team coaches Roy Aitken and Andy Watson both followed McLeish down to England after working alongside him in the Scotland camp.

Both are also former team-mates of McLeish at Aberdeen but bring their own management and coaching credentials to Blues' management set-up.

As a player, Aitken was a legend at Celtic before shorter spells at Newcastle United, St. Mirren and Aberdeen, where he then moved into management and led the Dons to the Scottish League Cup in 1995.

Aitken then moved to England and held jobs as assistant-manager at Leeds United and Aston Villa before his stint of office with the Scotland team, adding further international experience to the 57 caps he won as a player.

Watson had a lower profile playing career which took in spells at Leeds United, Hearts, Hibernian and Aberdeen before he launched his coaching career at Hibs.

McLeish then took him to Motherwell, Hibs, Rangers and Scotland and had no hesitation in calling on his knowledge again when putting together his backroom team at Birmingham.

Name: Roy Aitken
Born: Irvine, Scotland 24/11/58
Playing career: Celtic, Newcastle United, St. Mirren, Aberdeen
Coaching career: Aberdeen (manager), Leeds, Aston Villa, Scotland, Birmingham City

Name: Andy Watson
Born: Aberdeen, Scotland 03/09/59
Playing career: Leeds, Hearts, Hibernian, Aberdeen
Coaching career: Hibernian, Motherwell, Rangers, Scotland, Birmingham City

MARTIN
TAYLOR

JORDON
MUTCH

PRIZE GUYS

The Blues had little to celebrate collectively at the end of last season, but the team's outstanding individual performers were honoured for their efforts during the 2007/08 campaign.

Leading the way was winger Sebastian Larsson who swept the board in picking up six awards at the Blues traditional end-of-season bash at the Birmingham ICC.

The Swedish international was named as Player of the Year, Players' Player of the Year, Junior Blues' Player of the Year and BRMB listeners' Player of the Year.

Larsson's winning thunderbolt at Tottenham also earned him the Goal of the Season and Moment of the Season awards. Departing striker Mikael Forssell was a double winner as he picked up the prize for Top Goalscorer and a special award in recognition of scoring the Blues first Premier League hat-trick.

Stephen Kelly's consistency was rewarded with the Outstanding Achievement award after playing in every minute of Blues' Premier League campaign, while highly promising teenage midfielder Jordon Mutch was named as the Academy Player of the Year.

WORD SEARCH

FUN AND GAMES!

See if you can find the **16** words associated with Birmingham City in the wordsearch below…

```
C A R S L E Y W R O L Y A T R
B T N Y H P R U M Y K J R K E
C L T C B B T H L J R K M P F
D X U E C N R C O Z C Z N R E
K R N E D T C H B R H S L Y E
K T B Z S N N N L H A W P E E
M R N M V S E B S S M E V R Z
P K V O D N P D I P R L F Z
F I H N D X I Q T E I D N E M
S N T A V L B T Y L O N P E M
L L F C L W T T Q C N A D H G
L C A I H H R J N M S T M S R
M D H O N V J T K R H S Z C J
D P L F G P G Y Y M I T G M M
Y B D E F E N C E L P N F D L
```

Answers page 61

40

GARY
McSHEFFREY

MARCUS BENT
READY TO MAKE HIS MARC-US

"No league is easy and I know it's going to be a long, hard season but hopefully we'll be strong enough and good enough to go straight back up."

Blues' boss Alex McLeish made sure his new-look squad would not be short of firepower for their Championship challenge with some canny close-season shopping.

Marcus Bent was added to the roster of strikers when he joined the Blues from Charlton Athletic in a million-pound-plus deal.

With more than 100 career goals to his name, the experienced frontman certainly knows where the net is and proved that at St Andrew's last season when he bagged two for Wigan against the Blues.

The Latics were one of ten clubs Bent has previously played for since launching his career at Brentford and his services continued to be in demand when Wigan opted not to extend his loan spell from Charlton Athletic.

Blues' Championship rivals Cardiff City were close to clinching a deal for the former England under-21 international, who has also played top-flight football for Everton, Crystal Palace, Leicester City and Blackburn Rovers.

But when McLeish came calling Bent had no hesitation in signing a three-year deal at the Blues, where he is looking to repeat the promotion he previously enjoyed at Blackburn in 2001 alongside new Blues team-mates Martin Taylor and Damien Johnson.

"When Birmingham came in it was a lot more appealing because I think it's more likely that Birmingham are going to get into the Premier League," said Bent, who McLeish wanted to add a physical presence to Blues' front line.

"No league is easy and I know it's going to be a long, hard season but hopefully we'll be strong enough and good enough to go straight back up."

FACT FILE

Name: Marcus Bent
Born: 19 May, 1978, London
Position: Striker
Previous clubs: Brentford, Crystal Palace, Port Vale, Sheffield United, Blackburn Rovers, Ipswich Town, Leicester City (loan), Everton, Charlton Athletic, Wigan Athletic (loan)
Career goals: 107
Internationals: England U21

TARTAN TERRORS

Perhaps not surprisingly Alex McLeish's first two signings as the Blues' boss had strong Scottish connections with the Blues now benefiting from the presence of the Tartan terrors.

JAMES McFADDEN

In January 2007, Blues splashed out what could eventually add up to a club record £6 million fee to bring Everton forward James McFadden to St. Andrew's.

The former Motherwell man played under McLeish for Scotland where he took on legendary status last season when his stunning long-range strike gave the Scots a memorable 1-0 over France in Paris.

A famous winner against Holland in 2003 further underlined McFadden's love of the big stage, where he has forged a reputation for scoring spectacular goals.

Blues fans were given a taste of that last season when he scored a superb free-kick against Arsenal before keeping his cool later in the same game to equalise from the penalty spot.

Injuries restricted his impact as the Blues just failed to beat the drop but the 25-year-old's pace, trickery and eye for goal should make him a key part of McLeish's planned promotion jigsaw in the Championship.

FACT FILE

James McFadden
Born: 14 April, 1983 Glasgow
Position: Forward
Previous clubs: Motherwell, Everton
Country: Scotland

DAVID MURPHY

Alex McLeish raided former club Hibernian to land David Murphy in the transfer window during the 2007/08 season for a £1.5 million fee, although the left-back is not actually a Scot.

Born in Hartlepool, Murphy started his career along the road at Middlesbrough where he played a handful of games before being snapped up for Hibs in 2004 by former Boro stalwart Tony Mowbray.

Murphy played almost 150 times for the Edinburgh club, helping them to a third-placed finish in the Scottish Premier League and a triumph in the 2007 League Cup shortly before returning to England and St. Andrew's.

Playing 14 games in the Premier League for Blues, Murphy was first-choice left-back for McLeish and should have a key part to play in the back-four as the Blues look to bounce straight back to the top flight.

FACT FILE

David Murphy
Born: 1 March, 1984 Hartlepool
Position: Left-back
Previous clubs:
Middlesbrough, Hibs

UP FOR THE CUP

Blues did win one piece of silverware last season when the reserves lifted the Birmingham Senior Cup.

After overcoming local non-league sides Halesowen Town, Solihull Moors and Banbury United, the Blues faced Wolves in the semi-finals. A first goal in a Blues shirt from Argentinian striker Mauro Zarate gave the second string a 1-0 win to set up a final against Burton Albion. And Blues proved too strong for Nigel Clough's Blue Square Premier reserve side as they romped to a 5-0 win to take the trophy

at St. Andrew's. Garry O'Connor led the way with a hat-trick as Stuart Parnaby and Cameron Jerome also got themselves on the scoresheet for a powerful Blues line-up.

In the Premier Reserve League South, Blues finished seventh but will not play league football in 2008/09. Relegation for the first-team meant that the Blues reserves would have had to play in the Central League and Alex McCleish and reserves/Academy boss Terry Westley decided instead to play a series of friendlies to aid player development.

Premier Reserve League South 2007/08

1	Aston Villa Reserves (C)	18	10	5	3	38	17	+21	35
2	West Ham Utd. Reserves	18	9	4	5	32	21	+11	31
3	Reading Reserves	18	8	7	3	32	16	+16	31
4	Arsenal Reserves	18	8	6	4	26	17	+9	30
5	Fulham Reserves	18	8	4	6	27	25	+2	28
6	Chelsea Reserves	18	5	7	6	23	21	+2	22
7	Birmingham City Reserves	18	6	4	8	25	33	-8	22
8	Tottenham HS Reserves	18	5	6	7	22	24	-2	21
9	Portsmouth Reserves	18	5	4	9	12	25	-13	19
10	Derby County Reserves	18	1	3	14	13	51	-38	6

STUART
PARNABY

FUN & GAMES!

Guess Who?

All Messed Up!

1. EXAL SIEHLCM
2. RINTAM YOLRAT
3. VEKNI SLIPLPIH
4. SURAMC NETB
5. NOCIL YODEL
6. TARSUT YABPRNA
7. VADID PURMYH
8. EEL RASCELY

Answers page 61

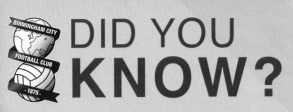

Enjoy these facts about the Blues...

- Blues took their current name as Birmingham City in 1943 after they had previously been known as Small Heath Alliance, Small Heath and Birmingham FC.

- Trevor Francis is Blues' youngest ever player after making his debut in 1970 at the age of 16 years and seven months. Francis then became the first £1 million player in England when he was sold to Nottingham Forest in 1978, returning to St. Andrew's in 1996 as manager.

- Blues were the first English club to play in European club football when they took part in the first Inter-Cities Fairs Cup in 1956. They were also the first English club to reach a European final, losing to Barcelona in 1960 and AS Roma in 1961 in the Inter-Cities Fairs Cup, which later became the Uefa Cup.

- In 1955 three teams finished level on points at the top of Division Two, but Blues were crowned champions thanks to their superior goal average, as it was then known.

- Current goalkeeper Maik Taylor has won the most international caps of any player while playing for Blues. Before the start of the 2007/08 season, he had won 39 caps for Northern Ireland during his time at St. Andrew's.

- The Blues' boss Alex McLeish received an honorary degree from the University of Aberdeen for his distinguished service to Scottish sport.

- The Blues joint first-team coach Roy Aitken was known as 'The Bear' during his playing days at Celtic because of his impressive physical presence in midfield.

- New Blues signing Lee Carsley was born in Birmingham, spent time at St. Andrew's as a junior and most members of his family are Blues fans.

- The record attendance at St Andrew's is 66,844 for an FA Cup fifth-round tie against Everton in February, 1939. The capacity now is just over 30,000.

STEPHEN
KELLY

MAZE

BLUES' HUNT FOR CHAMPIONSHIP GLORY

CAN YOU FIND YOUR WAY TO THE HEART OF THE MAZE AND LIFT THE CHAMPIONSHIP TROPHY?

Answers page 61

MAIK
TAYLOR

GOLDEN OLDIE

Goalkeeper Maik Taylor may be nearing the veteran stage but proving there's no substitute for experience the Blues number-one is still going strong.

Although the Blues suffered the drop last season, Taylor didn't let his standards slip as he regained first-choice status from Colin Doyle.

A string of impressive performances followed which meant that Liverpool were tracking the Northern Ireland international when his last Blues contract expired in the summer.

But rather than play second fiddle to Reds stopper Pepe Reina at Anfield, Taylor penned a new two-year deal at St. Andrew's to ensure that the Blues promotion challenge should be in safe hands.

"I still have a big desire to play and, as long as I keep my form and fitness, that's more likely here."

"I enjoy playing for Birmingham and although obviously it was tremendously disappointing to get relegated I am really optimistic about the future," Taylor said.

Previously a promotion winner with Fulham, Taylor has over 500 career games under his belt and McLeish is delighted to have that kind of experience to call on again.

"Maik is an excellent keeper and a fine athlete, who has kept himself in great condition," said McLeish.

FACT FILE

Name: Maik Taylor
Born: 4 September, 1971, Germany
Position: Goalkeeper
Previous clubs: Barnet, Southampton, Fulham, Birmingham City.
Club apps: 519
International caps: 67

F&C Investments
F&C Investments Expect excellence F&C Investments Expect excellence
BRING IT ON
F&C Investments Expect excellence F&C Investments
F&C Inv
mitre

BIRMINGHAM CITY
FOOTBALL CLUB
- 1875 -

MEHDI NAFTI
UP FOR THE FIGHT

"He gives everything in training and everything on a matchday. Mehdi is the type of player that I identify with and want to bring into the club."

Tough-tackling midfielder Mehdi Nafti has endured mixed fortunes since joining Blues but received some good news in the summer when boss Alex McLeish confirmed that he wanted the Tunisian international to form part of his new-look squad.

Nafti missed almost an entire season with a serious knee injury and experienced both promotion and relegation in his first three and a half years at St. Andrew's.

But his commitment to the cause has never wavered and that was reflected when McLeish took up the option to extend Nafti's contract by a further 12 months when his previous deal expired at the end of last season.

"He's a great character and brings a good spirit to the dressing room," said the Blues boss.

"He gives everything in training and everything on a matchday. Mehdi is the type of player that I identify with and want to bring into the club."

Nafti's combative style in the centre of midfield is sure to be a vital ingredient in Blues' quest to battle their way out of the Championship, which will hopefully mean a further upturn in fortunes for the Blues scrapper by the end of the season.

FACT FILE

Name: Mehdi Nafti
Born: 28 November, 1978, Tunisia
Position: Midfielder
Previous clubs: Toulouse, Racing Santander.

STEPHEN KELLY
RECORD BREAKER

"No other outfield player in the league could match Kelly's attendance record, as he was a first-choice pick in the Blues' back-four for both Steve Bruce and then Alex McLeish."

The Blues might have been unable to win their relegation fight last season, but it was still a memorable campaign for right-back Stephen Kelly.

Remarkable, Kelly played every single minute of the Blues' Premier League fixtures.

And in doing so, the ultra-consistent right-back became the most prolific performer in the top-flight.

No other outfield player in the league could match Kelly's attendance record, as he was a first-choice pick in the Blues' back-four for both Steve Bruce and then Alex McLeish.

Playing mainly at right-back, the former Tottenham defender steered clear of injury and suspension, picking up just three yellow cards, and never let his standards drop as he held off the competition for his place to be one of the first names on the team-sheet every week.

"I was proud to keep my place in the team for every Premier League game, because it was no easy feat," said Kelly.

"It's something I can be proud of because not many people get to achieve that."

FACT FILE

Name: Stephen Kelly
Born: 6 September, 1983
Position: Defender
Previous clubs: Tottenham Hotspur, Southend United (loan), QPR (loan), Watford (loan)
Country: Republic of Ireland

LIAM RIDGEWELL
TRUE BLUE

"It's up to all of us to give our all to get this club back in the Premier League where it belongs"

When Liam Ridgewell moved across Birmingham to join Blues from arch-rivals Aston Villa he bridged a 20-year gap.

A few fans might have raised their eyebrows when Ridgewell became the first player since Des Bremner in the mid-1980s to make such a move on a permanent basis.

But the young centre-back quickly became a true Blue thanks to a highly impressive first season at St. Andrew's.

Ridgewell missed just three league games in the 2007/08 campaign and captained the side on numerous occasions in the injury-enforced absence of Damien Johnson.

Relegation took some of the gloss off the former England under-21 international's debut year, but that set-back has only enhanced Ridgewell's desire to be a success in a Blue s shirt.

He will have a key part to play this season, along with central defensive colleagues Radhi Jaidi and Martin Taylor, as they look to provide a solid platform for a promotion push in the Championship.

And with several exciting new signings on board, Ridgewell is eager to make amends.

"It's up to all of us to give our all to get this club back in the Premier League where it belongs," he said.

"We were disappointed big-time to be relegated but that disappointment has been replaced by a hunger to get promoted back to the top-flight."

"We are a club that should be in the Premier League and we have got to do everything to make sure we get back there."

FACT FILE

Name: Liam Ridgewell
Born: 21 July, 1984, London
Position: Defender
Previous clubs: West Ham, Aston Villa.
Country: Republic of Ireland

SEB LARSSON
SUPER SWEDE

"In his first two seasons with the Blues, starting with a loan move from the Gunners, Larsson weighed in with an impressive 15 goals"

It's no wonder the Blues battled so hard in the summer to hold onto their Super Swede – Sebastian Larsson.

'Seb' had such an impressive season in the Premier League in 2007/08 that he was tracked by a number of top-flight clubs.

But with boss Alex McLeish keen to build a promotion-chasing squad around players like Larsson, the former Arsenal midfielder was offered a new deal at St. Andrew's.

In his first two seasons with the Blues, starting with a loan move from the Gunners, Larsson weighed in with an impressive 15 goals.

And it was invariably the quality of those goals that made him such a fans' favourite.

A free-kick specialist, Larsson added to his repertoire last season with three more stunning efforts and for the second year earned the Blues' goal-of-the-season award.

This time, though, his winning entry came from open play as he struck with a long-range screamer at Tottenham in injury-time to give McLeish a winning start as Blues' boss.

Larsson also helped Sweden qualify for Euro 2008 and played in the finals in Austria and Switzerland last summer before returning for pre-season training at the Blues.

Blues insisted that the winger would be staying, and if the predators are kept at bay for another 12 months, Larsson should light up the Championship to give himself the chance of performing on the big stage again.

FACT FILE

Name: Sebastian Larsson

Born: 6 June, 1985, Eskilstuna, Sweden.

Position: Midfielder

Previous clubs: IFK Eskilstuna, Arsenal.

Country: Sweden

MARTIN
TAYLOR

QUIZ ANSWERS

LET'S GET QUIZZICAL (Page 29)

1 Scotland
2 Mikael Forssell
3 Sebastian Larsson
4 Aston Villa and West Bromwich Albion
5 Republic of Ireland
6 Austria
7 Stephen Kelly
8 Wigan Athletic
9 Middlesbrough
10 Maik Taylor
11 Wast Hills
12 James McFadden

MAZE (Page 51)

WORDSEARCH (Page 40)

BENT
BLUES
CARSLEY
CHAMPIONSHIP
DEFENCE
GOALS
JOHNSON
MCFADDEN
MCLEISH
MCSHEFFREY
MURPHY
PHILLIPS
PITCH
REFEREE
STANDREWS
TAYLOR

ALL MESSED UP (Page 48)

EXAL SIEHLCM - Alex McLeish
RINTAM YOLRAT - Martin Taylor
VEKNI SLIPLPIH - Kevin Phillips
SURAMC NETB - Marcus Bent
NOCIL YODEL - Colin Doyle
TARSUT YABPRNA - Stuart Parnaby
VADID PURMYH - David Murphy
EEL RASCELY - Lee Carsley

GUESS WHO (Page 48)

1 Gary McSheffrey
2 Radhi Jaidi
3 James McFadden
4 Maik Taylor